*For Jo, with all my love.*
T. B.

*To Sam.*
R. B.

An Imprint of Sterling Publishing
387 Park Avenue South
New York, NY 10016

Text © 2004 by Tony Bonning
Illustrations © 2004 by Rosalind Beardshaw

This 2013 edition published by Sandy Creek.

ISBN 978-1-4351-4925-0

Manufactured in Heshan, China
Lot #:
2 4 6 8 10 9 7 5 3 1
10/13

# Kiss the Frog

Tony Bonning • Rosalind Beardshaw

Sandy Creek
NEW YORK

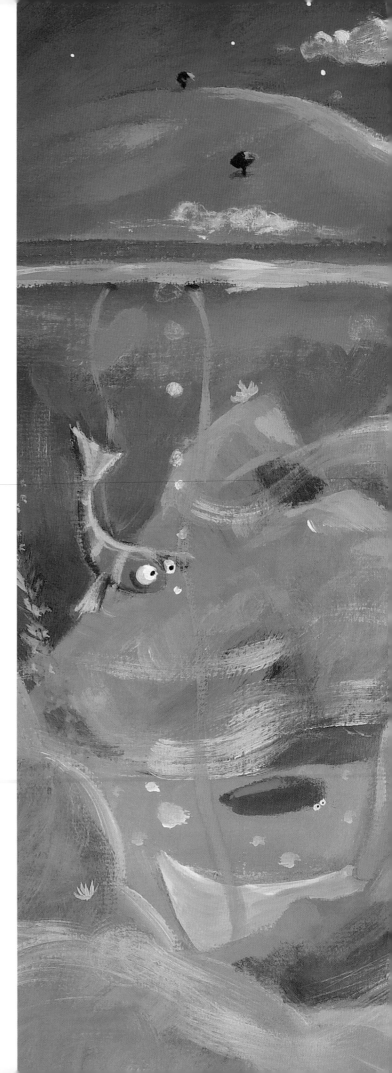

*B*eside a grand and
majestic castle was a pond,

and at the bottom
of this cool, clear pond
lived Snog the Frog.

Snog the Frog climbed on his log and said, "Today is Valentine's Day, and today I wish to feel like a prince. And to be a prince I need a kiss!"

With that in mind, he leapt onto the land and went

HOPPITY HOPPITY HOPPITY HOP,

until who should he meet, but Cow.

"Oh Cowy Cow Cow! I wish to feel like a prince. Pucker up your lovely lips and give me a kiss!"

"Who? You? Moo! No! Now go!"
"Oh! Just one?"
"No, go!"
And with that he went . . .

HOPPITY HOPPITY HOPPITY HOP,
until who should he meet, but Sheep.

"Oh Sheepy Sheep Sheep! I wish to feel like a
prince. Pucker those luscious lips and give me a kiss."
"Me? Meh! Baa! Nah! No!"
"Oh! Perhaps a peck?"
"Nooo, go!"

So with that, Snog the Frog went

HOPPITY

HOPPITY

HOPPITY HOP,

until who should he meet,
but Snake.

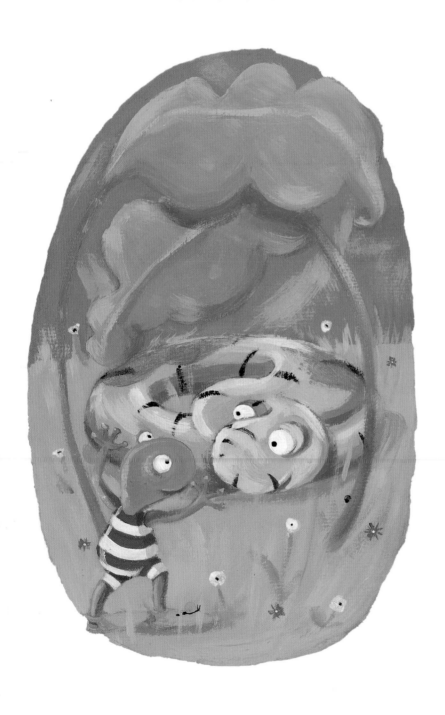

And with this, he went HOPPITY HOPPITY HOPPITY HOP, until who should he meet, but Pig.

"Oh Hoggy Hog Hog give this Froggy Frog Frog
a big wet kiss."
"What! Snort! I'd never kiss your sort."
"Spoilsport."

And with that, Snog the Frog went

HOPPITY

HOPPITY

HOPPITY HOP,

until who should he meet, but . . .

# ...Princess!

"Oh Princess, Your Highness, such happiness would I possess
were you to kiss me but once. Make me feel like a prince."
"Oh!" said the Princess, "I've read about this in the Fairy Tales.
One kiss and you turn into a prince."

And with this, she lifted Snog the Frog
and gave him a kiss.

"Alas, something is amiss.
The kiss has not turned you into a prince."
"Again, again, just one." The deed was done but . . .

**nothing!**

"Oh my!
Have one last try."
She did.

"I have tried once
and twice more since,
but you have not
become a prince."

**"No!"**
said Snog the Frog . . .